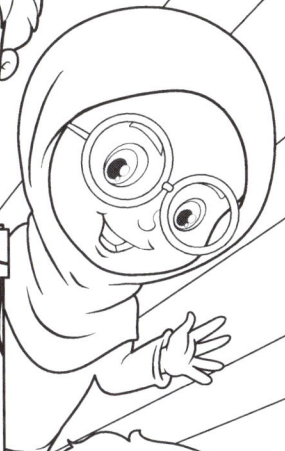

This Book Belongs To:

IDE

This Book Belongs To:

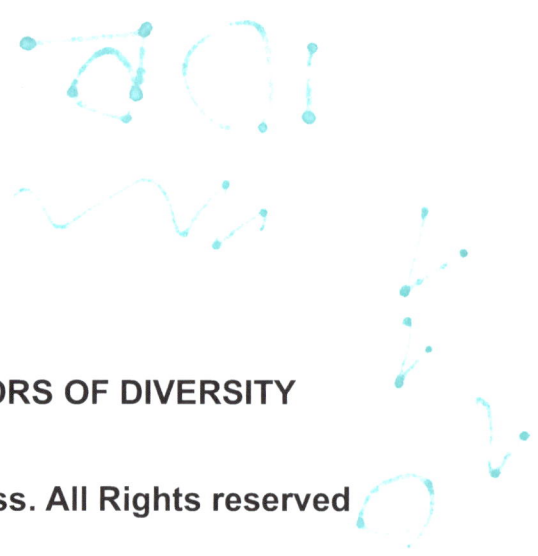

EQUALLY WONDERFUL! THE COLORS OF DIVERSITY

We live in a big, beautiful and diverse world

There are almost 8 Billion

PEOPLE IN OUR PLANET

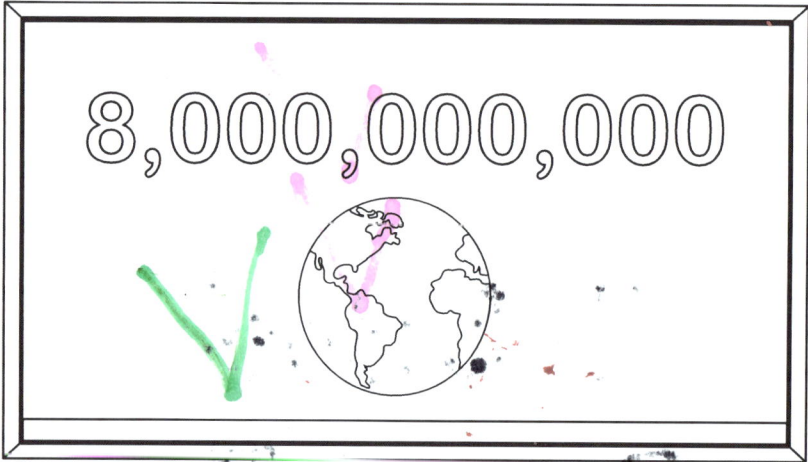

8,000,000,000

And people come in different sizes, shapes AND COLORS

We have different

SKIN COLORS

Olive Cinnamon Bronze

Cocoa Peach Chesnut Rose

Golden Chocolate Almond Ivory

Expresso Honey Beige Caramel

And they are all

Equally Beautiful

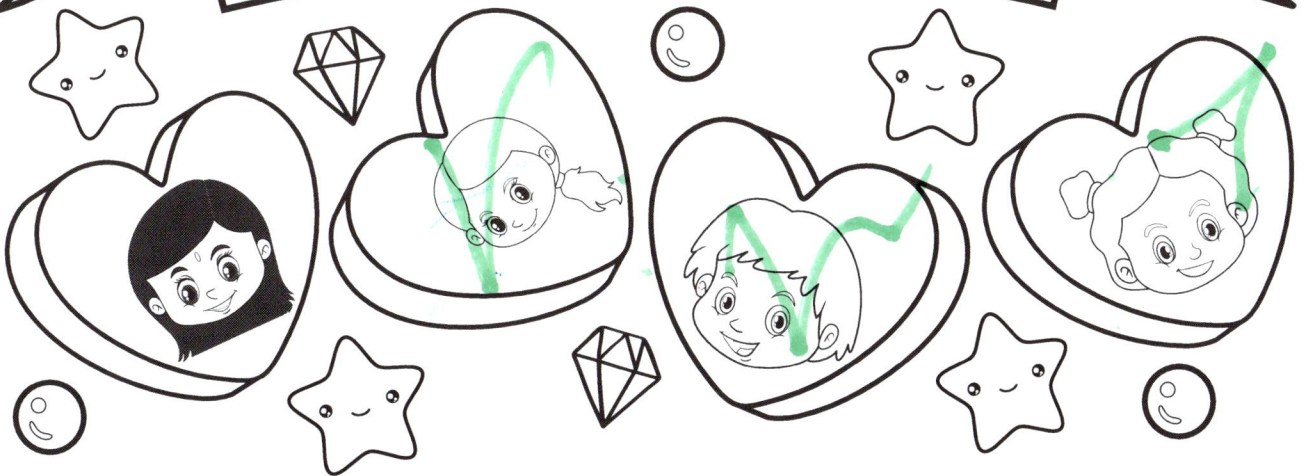

We have different KINDS OF HAIR

BLACK HAIR

BLONDE HAIR

CURLY HAIR

LONG HAIR

RED HAIR

BROWN HAIR

Or no hair at all

SHORT HAIR

THIN HAIR

THICK HAIR

STRAIGHT HAIR

WAVY HAIR

NO HAIR

How Amazing

We have different KINDS OF EYES AND NOSES

But we can see the same colors of the rainbow

And smell the same flowers and cookies

Some of us speak different languages

Or belong to different cultures

It's called
DIVERSITY

And diversity is a gift to be celebrated!

Imagine how boring it would be if everyone looked exactly the SAME

BEAUTY COMES IN ALL SHAPES, SIZES AND COLORS

We can look different
on the outside

Yet be the same
on the inside

We are like different flowers
FROM THE SAME GARDEN

KIND

and we can always choose
to speak words of kindness

And lift each other up

Higher and Higher

AT THE END OF THE DAY
we need to realize
what really matters

LOVE & KINDNESS

We share the same moon
we dance under the same sky
we glow under the same sun

We laugh when we are happy
WE CRY WHEN WE ARE SAD
In so many ways we are the same

And we all have the right
to be treated kindly

We all want to feel safe
We all deserve justice and peace
We are children!
WE ARE THE FUTURE!

WE ARE EQUALLY WONDERFUL

Made in the USA
Middletown, DE
19 November 2020